minedition

English editions published 2016 by Michael Neugebauer Publishing Ltd., Hong Kong

Text copyright for retelling © 2016 Lisbeth Zwerger
Illustrations copyright © 2016 Lisbeth Zwerger
Rights arranged with "minedition" Rights and Licensing AG, Zurich, Switzerland.
All rights reserved. This book, or parts thereof, may not be reproduced in any form without permission in writing from the publisher.
The scanning, uploading and distribution of this book via the Internet or via any other means without the permission of the publisher is illegal and punishable by law.
Please purchase only authorized electronic editions, and do not participate in or encourage electronic piracy of copyrighted materials.
Your support of the author's rights is appreciated.
Michael Neugebauer Publishing Ltd.,
Unit 23, 7F, Kowloon Bay Industrial Centre, 15 Wang Hoi Road, Kowloon Bay, Hong Kong.
Phone +852 2807 1711, e-mail: info@minedition.com
This edition was printed in July 2016 at L.Rex Printing Co Ltd.
3/F., Blue Box Factory Building, 25 Hing Wo Street, Tin Wan, Aberdeen, Hong Kong, China
Color separations by Pixelstorm, Vienna.
Library of Congress Cataloging-in-Publication Data available upon request.

ISBN 978-988-8341-28-3

10 9 8 7 6 5 4 3 2 1
First impression

For more information please visit our website: www.minedition.com

WILLIAM
SHAKESPEARE

ROMEO & JULIET

RETOLD AND ILLUSTRATED BY
LISBETH ZWERGER
TRANSLATED BY ANTHEA BELL

MINEDITION

Prologue

Two households, both alike in dignity,
In fair Verona, where we lay our scene,
From ancient grudge break to new mutiny,
Where civil blood makes civil hands unclean.
From forth the fatal loins of these two foes,
A pair of star-crossed lovers take their life,
Whose misadventured piteous overthrows
Doth with their death bury their parents' strife.
The fearful passage of their death-marked love
And the continuance of their parents' rage –
Which but their children's end, naught could remove –
Is now the two-hours' traffic of our stage,
The which, if you with patient ears attend,
What here shall miss, our toil shall strive to mend.

The beautiful city of Verona in Italy was in turmoil. Its citizens might well have lived harmoniously together, but two families were always disturbing the peace.

The Montagues were one of those families, the Capulets were the other. The enmity between them was ancient, and no one knew what had originally caused it. For the two families, however, and even their friends and their servants, that was of no importance. As soon as a Capulet set eyes on a Montague, he fell into a rage and went for the other man's throat. And the Montagues were no better. "We could give one of those Capulets a black eye again," one would say to another. "Yes, or make eyes at one of the Capulet girls," his friend would reply, and then they both laughed heartily.

The two families and their friends came to blows wherever they met, and even shed blood. There was an atmosphere of menace all over the city, and even Prince Escalus, who governed Verona, had failed to settle the quarrel. At last he lost patience, and decreed that the next man to offend by breaking the peace should die.

Romeo was the son of Count and Countess Montague. He was sixteen years old and head over heels in love with a lady called Rosaline. He longed for her, he dreamed of her, he yearned to hold her in his arms.

But how about Rosaline?
She thought nothing of him, she did not dream of him, and she certainly did not yearn to be held in his arms. She was entirely indifferent to Romeo.
His was a hopeless love!

Until recently, Romeo had enjoyed the company of his friends, but now he preferred to be by himself, walking gloomily along the streets of Verona. They wondered how to cheer him up.
His friends Benvolio and Mercutio had an idea: the Capulets, they told Romeo, were holding a great feast. "Come with us," they told him. "We'll slink in secretly, wearing masks, and you'll soon have something else to think about, because all the most beautiful women in Verona are invited!"
Romeo was not tempted; he wanted Rosaline and no one else.
"But Romeo," they told him, "Rosaline has been invited too!"

Welcome, gentlemen. Ladies that have their toes
Unplagued by corns will walk about with you.
Aha, my mistresses, which of you all
Will now deny to dance?
Act 1, Scene 5

Sure enough, the friends made their way into the house of their enemies the Capulets unrecognized. Everyone was in a merry mood, and dancing – only one young man was so melancholy that his feet were heavy as lead, and that was Romeo. Where was Rosaline? Where was the woman he loved?
Then Romeo's eyes fell on a young girl – and he forgot all about Rosaline.
How beautiful the girl was! How enchanting! Her eyes, her smile! He thought her face outshone the light of the torches.

Captivated, Romeo forgot where he was. He ought to have been on his guard here, in his arch-enemy's house, but he did not think of that. All he knew was that he must speak to the lovely girl he had seen. Romeo made his way through the crowd of dancers – and he was recognized by the quarrelsome Tybalt, Lord Capulet's nephew, who was famous for his readiness to pick a fight. "I know you as a Montague by your voice!" he cried, and turned to his page. "Fetch me my sword!"
Lord Capulet, a sensible man at heart, tried to calm his nephew. He wanted his feast to be a happy occasion, and even if a Montague had turned up, why should the guests be disturbed? Moreover, he had heard only good reports of Romeo.

Meanwhile, ignoring all the uproar, Romeo had managed to exchange a few words with the girl he had seen. They did not talk for long, but amazingly, every word shone brightly, every response seemed to sing as it flew through the air. And in the end, miraculously, they had even kissed.

His heart was beating wildly.

But who was the girl he adored? Suddenly someone called her, and she disappeared. Before the end of the feast, however, Romeo learned that he had fallen in love with the daughter of the Montagues' sworn enemies!

Romeo Montague loved Juliet Capulet!

'Tis but thy name that is my enemy.
Thou art thyself, though not a Montague.
Act 2, Scene 1

Juliet was not yet fourteen. Just before the beginning of the feast, her mother had come to her and said, "Juliet, you are still young, but you are old enough to think of marrying. Has that idea ever entered your head?"

It had never occurred to Juliet to think of marriage, but she had been born when her mother, Countess Capulet, was only fourteen herself; it was not unusual in those days.

"Count Paris, a rich young man from a distinguished family, has asked your father for your hand in marriage," her mother went on. "Pay him attention this evening."

None of this troubled Juliet at all. She was in love, and her love cast a golden light over everything. Who was the man who had cast such a spell on her?

Who was that handsome stranger? She had been called away from him before he could tell her his name.

But now she learned it. She had fallen in love with the son of her family's enemy! Juliet Capulet loved Romeo Montague.

Alas, what a terrible blow of fate!

Juliet was horrified. Her room had a little balcony, and she took refuge on it in her despair, crying out in the loneliness of the summer night, "O Romeo, Romeo, this cannot be true – surely you are no Montague and I am no Capulet!"

Little did she know that she was not really alone in the night. Romeo was standing just below her balcony, listening to every word she said. With his feelings in turmoil, he had parted from his friends on their way home, and inspired by his longing, he had climbed the Capulets' garden wall. Hearing Juliet, he plucked up his courage and replied, "Call me but love, and I'll be new baptized – henceforth I never will be Montague!"

Ah, how happy they both were! They poured out their hearts, knowing that they belonged together. Juliet adored Romeo. Romeo adored Juliet.

They opened their hearts to each other, exchanged vows, and talked of their love.

"My bounty is as boundless as the sea," Juliet cried "My love as deep – the more I give to thee, the more I have, for both are infinite."

"Three words, good Romeo, and good night indeed," she said as at last they parted.
"If you truly love me, and you are in earnest, if you truly want to marry me, then I will send my old nurse to see you tomorrow, and then you can tell her where and when the wedding is to be. And I shall lay my happiness at your feet."
"Good night," they promised one another. "Good night."
And so it was decided. Romeo and Juliet would marry the next day.

But come, young waverer, come, go with me.
In one respect I'll thy assistant be.
Act 2, Scene 2

Romeo could not sleep that night. Before dawn he was at the cell of his spiritual adviser Friar Laurence. The friar had been his friend since he was a child, and not long ago Romeo had told the holy man all about his unhappy love for Rosaline.

Indeed, Friar Laurence was rather surprised to find that Romeo had changed his mind so soon, and was in love with someone else.
Could this end well?
Could Romeo, who had loved Rosaline so passionately before, be serious in his new love for Juliet?
However, the friar had a sound reason for agreeing to marry the young couple. Given a little luck, he thought, this marriage might end the old enmity of the Capulet and Montague families. Good. He would marry Romeo and Juliet that very afternoon.
As Juliet had planned, her old nurse went to see Romeo at nine o'clock in the morning, and went back to her young mistress with the good news that Friar Laurence was prepared to marry the young lovers that same day!

Come, come with me, and we will make short work,
For, by your leaves, you shall not stay alone
Till Holy Church incorporate two in one. Act 2, Scene 5

Headstrong Romeo! He was so happy to hear the news.
As he waited for his bride to arrive, Friar Laurence warned him to love moderately,
for, he said, "These violent delights have violent ends."

Then Juliet herself appeared.
The ceremony was soon performed, and now the lovers were man and wife! Their
marriage, however, could not be acknowledged yet. Only under cover of darkness was
Romeo to visit his wife that night. The nurse would let down a rope ladder from the
balcony.
How long the day would seem!

I pray thee, good Mercutio, let's retire.
The day is hot, the Capels are abroad,
And if we meet we shall not scape a brawl,
For now, these hot days, is the mad blood stirring. Act 3, Scene 1

The summer sun blazed down on Verona. Romeo's cousin Benvolio and his friend
Mercutio were crossing a square in the heat when a crowd of young Capulets came
up, obviously with mischief in mind. Their leader was Juliet's cousin Tybalt. We have
met him before – a quarrelsome, hot-tempered young man. He was looking for Romeo
to call him out for his appearance at the Capulets' feast.
Romeo appeared, deep in thought. No one here, none of the belligerent young
Capulets knew his secret – he had just married Juliet! And although Tybalt did not
know it, Romeo had no intention of quarrelling with him, of all people, the cousin of
his beloved Juliet.

But his peaceful intentions did no good. Mercutio, knowing nothing of Romeo's change of mind, embarked on a furious argument with Tybalt. They both drew their swords, and with much shouting and bandying of words the fight grew ever fiercer, until Mercutio, struck by a mortal sword-thust, fell to the ground. Romeo was beside himself.

The new link between him and the Capulets was forgotten, all thought of reconciliation was gone! Tybalt had killed his friend, and was now his enemy. Revenge! Romeo rushed toward him, and after a short but ferocious fight, Tybalt fell dead. And Romeo was his murderer!

He must flee, for had not Prince Escalus, who ruled Verona, threatened anyone who disturbed the peace with death? Who would believe Romeo if he said that the murdered man had begun the fight?

Go, get thee to thy love, as was decreed.
Ascend her chamber, hence and comfort her.
Act 3, Scene 3

The world seemed to be holding its breath. All was lost.
Juliet was weeping in her room.
Romeo was shedding tears in Friar Laurence's cell.

But Friar Laurence believed good would prevail, and he encouraged Romeo.
"Romeo, you are alive. Tybalt was going to kill you, but you are alive. And so is Juliet – so let us rejoice!

"You thought you would be sentenced to death, but it has been announced that Prince Escalus is only sending you into exile. Is that not fortunate as well? You must leave Verona for the time being, but surely a time will come when you may return. Ride to Mantua early tomorrow morning and wait there for better times. But first, go to Juliet and comfort her."

Wilt thou be gone? It is not yet near day.
It was the nightingale, and not the lark,
That pierced the fearful hollow of thine ear.
Act 3, Scene 5

So what was that night like?

It was certainly the most wonderful night that Romeo and Juliet had ever known.

And like all wonderful experiences, it was over too soon.

When the lovers awoke, day was beginning to dawn, and a bird was singing its morning song outside the room. If only it had been a nocturnal song – they longed to spend more time together. But then they heard the quick footsteps of Juliet's nurse, and heard her warning voice. "Lord and Lady Capulet are on their way here!"

"Goodbye, dear Juliet."

"Goodbye, dear Romeo."

"Send messages every day, every hour, to tell me how you are."

"Farewell."

"Farewell."

Well, well, thou hast a careful father, child;
One who, to put thee from thy heaviness,
Hast sorted out a sudden day of joy,
That thou expect'st not, nor I looked not for.
Act 3, Scene 5

Juliet's parents entered her room in furious haste that morning. Full of hatred for the Montagues, they were making plans to avenge Tybalt's death: they were going to send a man to Mantua to poison his killer Romeo.

But now events took an alarming turn; the Capulets had decided to have their daughter's wedding to Count Paris celebrated in two days' time! It was to be a joyful occasion to help them to recover from their grief at the death of Tybalt. Juliet's parents could not understand her reluctance.

They said she should be grateful to be marrying such a noble young gentleman as Paris!

"Pull yourself together, girl," her father told her, "or I myself will drag you to the church." Even the old nurse who had been faithful to her since her early childhood let her down now, and advised her to marry Paris, saying he was the better choice – as if she were not married already!

Juliet felt as if everyone had forsaken her.

Hold, daughter, I do spy a kind of hope
Which craves as desperate an execution
As that is desperate which we would prevent.
Act 4, Scene 1

In despair, Juliet pretended she was going to confess her sins to Friar Laurence, the last friend she had in Verona. He had already heard of her misfortune; Count Paris himself had just been to the friar's cell to discuss the wedding.

Juliet, meeting him, was beside herself. No, she would never marry the Count. She would rather jump off the top of a tower, she said, give herself up to thieves, throw herself into a pit of snakes or let herself be chained to ferocious bears; she would sooner spend the night in a morgue full of rattling skeletons, moldering bones, and yellow skulls with no teeth left in their jaws! She would even prefer to throw herself into a freshly dug grave, wrapped in a dead man's shroud

But Friar Laurence had an idea that might come to their aid. It was a dangerous plan, and Juliet would have to summon up all her courage.

"When you go home," he told her, "pretend that everything is all right. Seem cheerful, as if you had nothing against the idea of marrying Paris. You must be a good actress. And make sure that your old nurse does not sleep in your room tomorrow night."

Juliet promised to do as the friar said.

"Here is a little flask," he went on. "Lie down in your bed tomorrow evening and drink the distilled herbal liquid in it. It will send you into a deep sleep, a trance that seems like death itself. Your lips and cheeks will turn pale, no one will be able to feel your pulse or your breath, you will lie there like the dead. And in the morning you will be found lifeless in your room, and they will take you not to the altar to be married, but to the family's burial vault. After 42 hours, however, you will awaken as if you had been sleeping. At that time Romeo will be with you, and take you to Mantua with him. I'll send a messenger to tell him our plan."

Juliet was a brave girl, and would do anything, however dangerous, for the sake of her beloved Romeo.

We shall be much unfurnished for this time.
What, is my daughter gone to Friar Laurence?
Act 4, Scene 2

All was topsy-turvy at the Capulets' house: the wedding guests had to be invited in a hurry, and twenty cooks were hired to prepare the wedding feast. Lord and Lady Capulet had their hands full.

Then Juliet appeared, asking her father to forgive her for her obstinacy.
Friar Laurence, she told him, had brought her to see reason when she went to make her confession to him, and now all was well. She would be happy for her wedding to Paris to be celebrated next day. Accompanied by her mother and her old nurse, Juliet went to her room to choose her best dress and most precious jewels to wear for the ceremony. Then she sent Lady Capulet and the nurse away, lay down – and drank the potion in Friar Laurence's flask at a single draft.

At the same time Friar Laurence himself, sitting in his cell, was writing Romeo a letter:

> *I write in haste, Romeo. Much has happened here, but all will be well.*
> *Come to the Capulets' burial vault tomorrow night. You will find Juliet there,*
> *fast asleep. Never fear, she is well! She took a sleeping draft and will wake at*
> *about the time of your arrival. Get on your horse and ride straight back with*
> *her to Mantua. She will tell you what has happened. Both of you must stay in*
> *Mantua and be happy. Here in Verona, I will work to make it possible for you*
> *to return. God be with you!*

Friar Laurence gave the letter to his friend Friar John, telling him to set off for Mantua at once, and give the news in the letter to Romeo Montague.

Unhappy fortune! By my brotherhood,
The letter was not light, but full of charge,
Of much import, and the neglecting it
May do much danger.
Act 5, Scene 2

Friar John hurried away, with Friar Laurence's letter in his baggage. He did not want to set off for Mantua alone, so he joined another friar whose task was tending the sick, for there was a terrible pestilence raging in the country around Verona at that time. But when the two friars entered the house of a man with a severe case of the pestilence, the officers who went around to isolate anyone who had been in touch with the sick, so as to keep the infection from spreading, unexpectedly appeared and sealed up the door, with the two friars inside.

Now they could not go on to Mantua, but Friar John kept calm. He had plenty to do here in the sick man's house. He did not know what was in Friar Laurence's letter, or how important it was.

All things that we ordainèd festival
Turn from their office to black funeral.
Our instruments to melancholy bells,
Our wedding cheer to a sad funeral feast;
Our solemn hymns to sullen dirges change;
Our bridal flowers serve for a buried corpse,
And all things change them to the contrary.
Act 4, Scene 5

Busy preparations for the wedding went on all night in the Capulets' house. There was so much to be done! Wood must be brought for the great hearth, spits for the roast meat, fruits, spices, all must be ready for the wedding feast. Soon the musicians, too, arrived to tune their instruments.

Early in the morning, the nurse went to help Juliet to dress and get ready. Juliet seemed to be sleeping very deeply, and simply could not be wakened. The nurse shook her, but in vain. Now she saw how pale the girl's face looked – and it was strange that she had gone to bed fully clothed. The nurse cried out loud for help. Juliet's mother and father came running in, and what weeping and lamentation there was! Their child was dead. It was all over. Juliet had died on the eve of her wedding. Now Friar Laurence arrived. He had to conduct not a marriage service but a funeral, and grief descended like a black cloth on the Capulet house. Only the musicians went on tuning up and making jokes.

I dreamt my lady came and found me dead –
Strange dream, that gives a dead man leave to think!
Act 5, Scene 1

The Capulets' funeral procession was observed by Romeo's servant, a young man called Balthasar, who was horrified, and set off for Mantua. He must let his master know about this dreadful misfortune at once.

When Romeo saw Balthasar coming, his heart lifted. He joyfully ran to meet him. "How are matters in Verona? How is my Juliet?" he asked.

Balthasar summoned up all his courage, and told Romeo what he had seen: Juliet was dead, and lying in the burial vault of the Capulets.

All attempts to console Romeo were useless.

Balthasar urged his master to compose himself, but in vain. Romeo sent him away, and told him to hire horses. He meant to ride back to Verona that same night.

When Balthasar was out of sight, Romeo went to visit an apothecary who was obviously in need of money. A stuffed alligator hung from the ceiling of his shop, with the skins of misshapen fishes, and there was a thick layer of dust on the shelves. But the only thing that Romeo wanted here was poison.

He persuaded the apothecary to sell him a little bottle of the deadly substance for forty gold ducats.

Here, here will I remain
With worms that are thy chambermaids. O, here
Will I set up my everlasting rest,
And shake the yoke of inauspicious stars
From this world-wearied flesh.
Act 5, Scene 3

Verona was usually fast asleep at this time of night, but there was some unrest in the streets. Several men who knew nothing about each other were coming from different directions to the same place; the family vault of the Capulets.

Paris, the unfortunate bridegroom, was the first to arrive. He wanted to bring flowers for his bride Juliet where she lay on her bier.

Then he heard footsteps. He quickly hid in the darkness and saw that Romeo Montague was approaching the vault, with tools and a lighted torch.

Paris held his breath: the exiled man, the enemy of the Capulets, the murderer of Tybalt was about to desecrate a grave as well, and disturb his bride's rest. He rushed out of hiding and attacked Romeo. Romeo wanted nothing less than to fight. But when Paris would not let him approach the vault, and his beloved Juliet, he too drew his sword. They had not been fighting for long before Paris sank lifeless to the ground beside the vault.

At last Romeo was in the vault with Juliet. Her beauty was still overwhelming.
He wished to be united with her at last in death – he had been unable to think of
anything else since the previous day. He embraced and kissed her one last time,
and then drank the poison in the little flask down to the very last drop.
"O true apothecary," he cried, "thus with a kiss I die!" And, kissing Juliet for the last
time, he fell dead–lifeless.

And now Friar Laurence arrived... ah, if only he had come a few minutes earlier!
He called to Romeo, but it was too late. Romeo was lying dead beside Juliet.

Juliet, that brave girl, was just awakening from her deep sleep.
Full of hope, she looked around. Yes, now she remembered: she was in her family's
burial vault. But where was Romeo?
Only now did she see him lying beside her.
Was he asleep?

Poor Friar Laurence could hardly bear it. He begged Juliet to leave the vault with
him at once. But suddenly, excited voices were heard, there was a tumult outside
the vault, and Father Laurence hurried out.

When Juliet saw that her beloved Romeo was dead, she no longer wanted to live herself. All hope was gone, so what was life still worth? To her sorrow, none of the poison
that Romeo had drunk was left, so she took his dagger and ended her life with it.

A glooming peace this morning with it brings.
The sun for sorrow will not show his head.
Go hence, to have more talk of these sad things.
Some shall be pardoned, and some punishèd.
For never was a story of more woe
Than this of Juliet and her Romeo.
Act 5, Scene 3

Guards, summoned by Balthasar and the unfortunate Paris's page, came running in and saw the tragic scene. But too late: nothing could be done for the lovers now!

Prince Escalus, the governor of Verona, also arrived. So did the parents of Romeo and Juliet, who had been awoken from sleep by the shouting in the streets. Breathless, they made their way to the vault, and faced the dreadful sight that met their eyes.

Half crazed with grief, the two hostile families stood side by side. How could what had happened be explained?
Mysteriously, Juliet had been dead for some time, but she was lying in the vault covered with blood. The dagger that had killed her was lying on the back of Romeo's body, so he could not have been her murderer.

Their parents could not grasp the full extent of the tragedy.

They knew nothing about the love between their children, or their marriage, or Tybalt's attack on Romeo. All the young couple's feelings and desperate plans of their son and daughter had been concealed from them. Only Friar Laurence could unravel the course of events, and tell them how he had tried in vain to put matters right.

He told them about the ardent love of Romeo and Juliet for one another, and spoke of his own hope that their love might have united the houses of Capulet and Montague in peace.

Sad and sorrowful, the parents stood by the grave where their children lay.
What had been the reason for the enmity between the two families?
It made no difference – there must be an end to it. Their remorse was too late, but now, at least, they would do what was right.
The parents of Romeo and Juliet took each other's hands. They decided to erect a memorial to their children, who had fallen victim to their deadly enmity. It would be a statue of pure gold.

From that day on, peace reigned in Verona. But at what a price?

Is that what really happened?

Is it what we want to believe?

Might the story not have taken a different turn?

Maybe Friar John reached Mantua after all,
and gave Friar Laurence's letter to Romeo?

Surely it was like that!

Romeo read the letter, borrowed a horse, and rode
as fast as he could to Verona and the Capulets'
burial vault.

He was alone in the graveyard. Paris had come an
hour earlier to lay flowers in his bride's tomb, and
had then gone away again. Undisturbed, Romeo
made his way into the vault, and waited. Sure enough,
Juliet opened her eyes and saw Romeo. And it all
turned out just as Friar Laurence had predicted.

If only...

L.Z.

Translator's note:

Romeo and Juliet, with its touching theme of two young people from hostile families who fall passionately in love, and then die tragically, has always been one of Shakespeare's most popular plays. He wrote it in the mid-1590s, and an early version first appeared in print in 1597. Its fast-moving action and wealth of poetic language make it as much of a favorite as ever today, 400 years after Shakespeare's death. In this book, Lisbeth Zwerger's retelling accompanied by her art beautifully illustrates the sad story.

Anthea Bell

The following titles were illustrated by Lisbeth Zwerger and have appeared in the Michael Neugebauer Edition:

Alice in Wonderland, Lewis Carroll
Dwarf Nose, Wilhelm Hauff
Tales From The Brothers Grimm, The Brothers Grimm
The Canterville Ghost, Oscar Wilde
The Little Mermaid, Hans Christian Andersen
The Merry Pranks Of Till Eulenspiegel, Heinz Janisch
The Night Before Christmas, Clement Clark Moore
The Pied Piper of Hamelin, The Brothers Grimm
The Selfish Giant, Oscar Wilde